This book is for the Peregrines class at
Gastrells Community Primary School, 2017.
Thank you all for your great pictures!

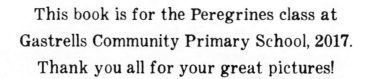

BLOOMSBURY CHILDREN'S BOOKS
Bloomsbury Publishing Inc., part of Bloomsbury Publishing Plc
1385 Broadway, New York, NY 10018

BLOOMSBURY, BLOOMSBURY CHILDREN'S BOOKS, and the Diana logo are trademarks of Bloomsbury Publishing Plc

First published in Great Britain in July 2018 by Bloomsbury Publishing Plc
Published in the United States of America in September 2019 by Bloomsbury Children's Books
Paperback edition published in August 2021

Bloomsbury books may be purchased for business or promotional use. For information on bulk purchases please contact
Macmillan Corporate and Premium Sales Department at specialmarkets@macmillan.com

ISBN 978-1-5476-0724-2 (paperback)

LCCN of hardcover edition: 2019006371

Art created digitally using Kyle T. Webster's natural media brushes for Photoshop and a selection of hand-painted textures
Typeset in Appareo Medium • Book design by Goldy Broad
Printed in China by Leo Paper Products, Heshan, Guangdong
4 6 8 10 9 7 5 3

To find out more about our authors and books visit www.bloomsbury.com and sign up for our newsletters.

RUBY
FINDS A
WORRY

TOM PERCIVAL

BLOOMSBURY
CHILDREN'S BOOKS
NEW YORK LONDON OXFORD NEW DELHI SYDNEY

Ruby loved being
Ruby.

She loved to swing up high . . .

. . . and she loved to explore
wild, faraway places.

Sometimes she even went all
the way to the very
bottom of the garden!

Ruby was perfectly happy.
Until one day . . .

. . . she discovered
a Worry.

It wasn't a very
big Worry . . .

In fact, it was so small that, at first,
Ruby hardly noticed it.

But then the Worry
started to grow.

Each day it got a little bit bigger . . .

It just wouldn't leave her alone.

It was there at breakfast, staring at her over the cereal box.

And it was STILL there at night, when she brushed her teeth.

The funny thing was that no one else could
see Ruby's Worry—not even her teacher.

So Ruby pretended that *she* couldn't see it either.

She *tried* to carry on as if everything was normal— but it just wasn't!

The Worry was *always* there—stopping her from doing the things that she loved.

Ruby wondered if the Worry
would ever go away.

What if it
didn't?

What if it stayed with her *forever*?

Ruby didn't realize it, but she was doing the worst thing you can ever do with a Worry:

she was worrying about it!

Now the Worry was
ENORMOUS!

It could barely fit in the
kitchen at dinnertime.

It filled up half the school bus . . .

. . . and it took up whole rows at the movie theater.

The Worry became the only thing that Ruby could think about, and it seemed like she would never feel happy again.

Then, one day, something unexpected happened . . .

Ruby noticed a boy sitting alone at the park.
He looked how she felt—sad.

And then she noticed something else, something
hovering next to him. Could it be . . .

a Worry?

It was!

Ruby realized that she wasn't the *only* person with a Worry after all.

Other people had them too!

She asked the boy what was on his mind
and, as he told her, the strangest
thing happened . . .

His Worry began to shrink!

Then Ruby did the best thing you can *ever* do if you have a Worry:

she talked about it.

As the words tumbled out, Ruby's Worry began to shrink until it was barely there at all.

Soon, both of their Worries were gone!

Finally, Ruby felt like herself again!

Of course, that wasn't the last time
she ever had a Worry (everyone gets
them from time to time).

But now that she knew how to
get rid of them . . .

. . . they never hung around for long.